To the child I write for—
the one who sits, watches,
and waits for me to hand over the story.
Thank you for staying with me.
—C.D.B.

To my Dad.
—F.C.

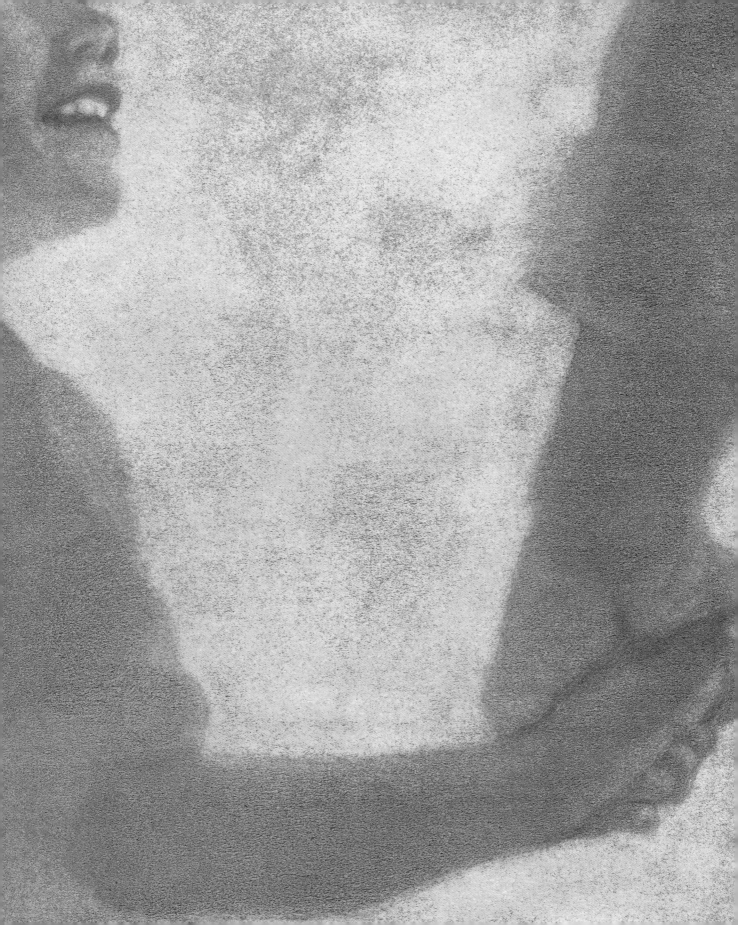

Daddy, Daddy, Be There

CANDY DAWSON BOYD
FLOYD COOPER

The Putnam & Grosset Group

Daddy, Daddy,
Be there.
Put your hand out to me
In scary crowds,
On first school days
And roller-coaster rides.
Daddy, Daddy,
Be there.

Daddy, Daddy,
Be there,
When my questions need your ears, listening,
Your eyes, searching,
And your heart, loving me.
Tell me I am smart,
Tell me I am special,
Tell me I am able
With your ears, eyes, and heart.
Daddy, Daddy,
Be there.

Daddy, Daddy,
Be there.
Point out the pictures in my storybooks,
Read the nursery rhymes to me,
Show me your daddy, your mama, your growing up.
Share a cookie, half a sandwich, a joke,
Share your music, your dreams.
I'll listen with my heart as best I can.
Daddy, Daddy,
Be there.

Daddy, Daddy,
Be there.
Hug Mama and smile at her
On Tuesdays and in the grocery store.
Kiss us and take our pictures
At picnics and on birthdays.
Tell us big and little stories.
Daddy, Daddy,
Be there.

Daddy, Daddy,
Be there,
Not only on weekends or across telephone lines,
Not only during commercials or between innings.
Share surprises, the only one-time times.
Shout when I slide into home base
Or sing solo in the school choir.
Daddy, Daddy,
Be there.

Daddy, Daddy,
Be there.
Plant new trees and flower bulbs,
And a red rose bush for Mama.
Play inside and outside games with me,
Flick water drops and light campfires,
Dive into cold waves,
Slide down snowy hillsides
With me.
Daddy, Daddy,
Be there.

Daddy, Daddy,
Be there.
Trains speed by,
Planes lift off,
Cars race around,
Trucks inch forward,
Ships sail away,
Teachers change classes,
Grandpas, grandmas, aunts, uncles die,
Sometimes even sisters, brothers, and best friends.
Big people separate and divorce.
See what I see.
Daddy, Daddy,
Be there.

Daddy, Daddy,
Be there.
I heard you holler
About money and bills.
I saw you push Mama
And take another drink
And turn the television up,
Then leave, slam the door shut.
I feel the holler, the push, the door slammed.
Please stop. Stop, please. Please. Stop.
Make home safe.
Daddy, Daddy,
Be there.

Daddy, Daddy,
Be there.
Don't let the world knock you out
And drag you off.
No matter what, struggle back home,
Take my hand,
Let me be your friend.
Do the tough work.
Get well and strong.
Daddy, Daddy,
Be there.

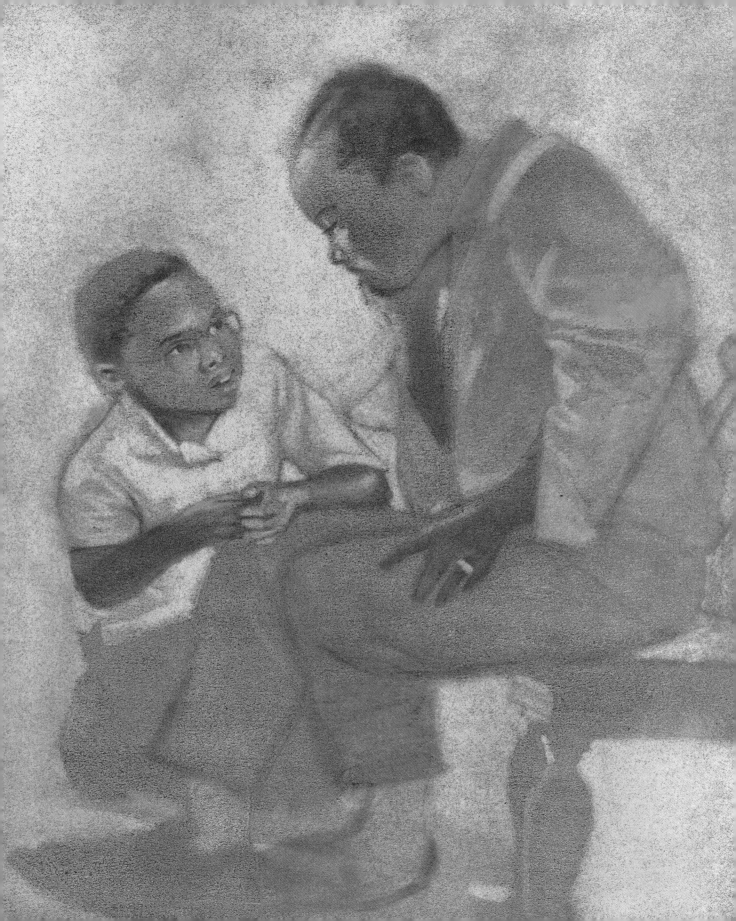

Daddy, Daddy,
Be there.
If we live where you and Mama stay gone,
Letting sitters or private schools raise me,
If we live where everyone works
But there is always barely just enough,
And no one sees me,
And feelings end up stuffed in a box,
Find a way to save us.
Make a family.
Daddy, Daddy,
Be there.

Daddy, Daddy,
Be there,
During the hard times when the money goes,
During the bread-and-brown-sugar-breakfast mornings,
During the saxophone-blowing-blues nights,
During the in-between, weary working months,
During the string of long years,
Daddy, Daddy,
Be there.

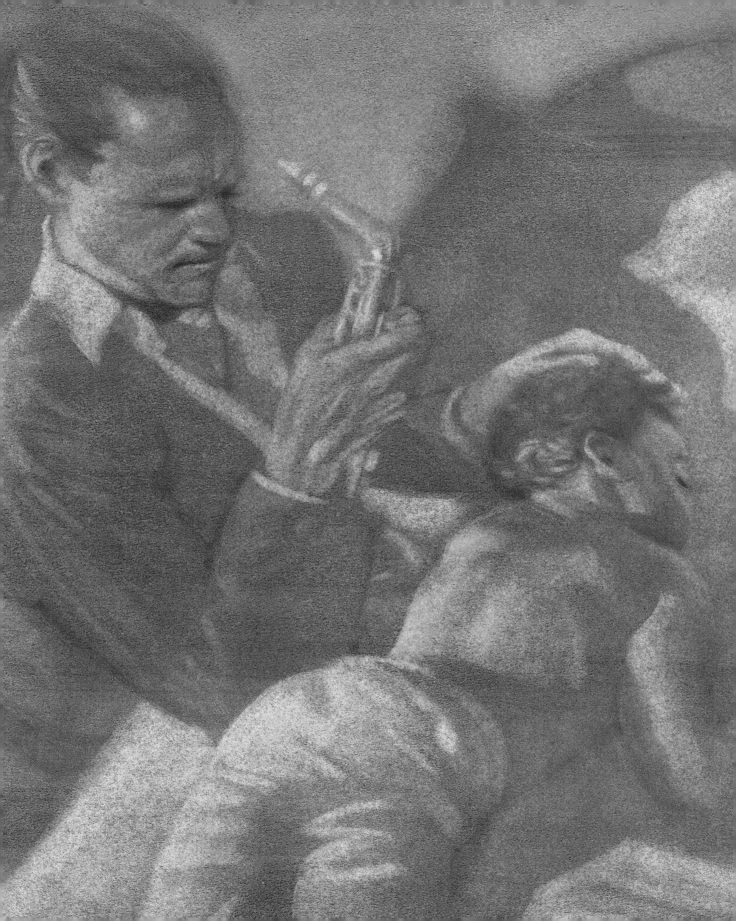

Daddy, Daddy,
Be there,
When others gather,
When they tell family stories,
When one someone says to me:
"What's your daddy like?"
Who you are and what you are,
Who you are and where you are
Will answer!
Daddy, Daddy,
Be there.

Daddy, Daddy,
Be there,
When I dye my hair green or cut it off
Or pierce my ears and nose,
When my music rocks the house.
But grab me when I wander too far from home,
Too close to a danger I cannot see.
Daddy, Daddy,
Be there.

Daddy, Daddy,
Be there,
With a firm hand and confident grin,
When I take off without you,
When I graduate, head high,
When I enter a new world,
One you helped me reach,
One you could never enter.
Daddy, Daddy,
Be there.

Daddy, Daddy,
Be there,
As I swim mountain lakes,
Stride across deserts,
Stretch to the sun and moon and stars,

Build doors and rooms
And skyscrapers and worlds.
No matter what, Daddy, I'll know
That you are there, close by.
My Daddy, Daddy,
There.

Daddy, Daddy,
Be there.
Let me sit with you,
Let me hold your spotted hand.
Let my eyes be yours, and my ears as well.
I will remember when you were there for me
And asked for nothing in return.
Now I am here for you.
Daddy, Daddy,
I love you.

Printed on recycled paper

Text copyright © 1995 by Candy Dawson Boyd
Illustrations copyright © 1995 by Floyd Cooper
All rights reserved. This book, or parts thereof, may not be reproduced
in any form without permission in writing from the publisher.
A PaperStar Book, published in 1998 by The Putnam & Grosset Group,
200 Madison Avenue, New York, NY 10016. PaperStar is a registered
trademark of The Putnam Berkley Group, Inc. The PaperStar logo is
a trademark of The Putnam Berkley Group, Inc.
Originally published in 1995 by Philomel Books.
Published simultaneously in Canada. Printed in the United States of America.
Book design by Cecilia Yung and Donna Mark.
The text is set in Trump Mediaeval.
Library of Congress Cataloging-in-Publication Data
Boyd, Candy Dawson. Daddy, Daddy, be there / Candy Dawson Boyd;
illustrated by Floyd Cooper.   p.   cm.   1. Father and child—Juvenile literature.
[1. Father and child.]   I. Cooper, Floyd, ill.   II. Title.   HQ755.85.B69   1995
306.874'2—dc20   94-8876   CIP   AC
ISBN 0-698-11750-6
1   3   5   7   9   10   8   6   4   2